8/11

DATE DUE

NOV - 1 2011	

For little John
Davide

To valentina
gianluca

First published in Australia and New Zealand in 2010 by
Wilkins Farago Pty Ltd, PO Box 78, Albert Park, Victoria 3206, Australia

Teachers' Notes and other downloads at **www.wilkinsfarago.com.au**

First edition published in Italy by ZOOlibri in 2008
Original edition's title: "L'Orso con la spada"
Text and illustrations Copyright © ZOOlibri, Reggio Emilia, Italia.
All rights reserved.

National Library of Australia Cataloguing-in-Publication entry:

Author: Cali, Davide.
Title: The bear with the sword / Davide Cali ;
illustrator, Gianluca Foli.
ISBN: 9780980607048 (hbk.)
Target Audience: For primary school age.
Subjects: Bears--Juvenile fiction.
Environmental degradation--Juvenile
fiction.
Dewey Number: A823.4

Printed in China by Everbest Printing
Distributed by Tower Books (Australia) and Addenda Publishing (New Zealand)

FSC
Mixed Sources
Product group from well-managed
forests and other controlled sources
Cert no. SGS-COC-003563
www.fsc.org
© 1996 Forest Stewardship Council

The Bear with the Sword

Davide Cali • Gianluca Foli

wf
WILKINSfarago

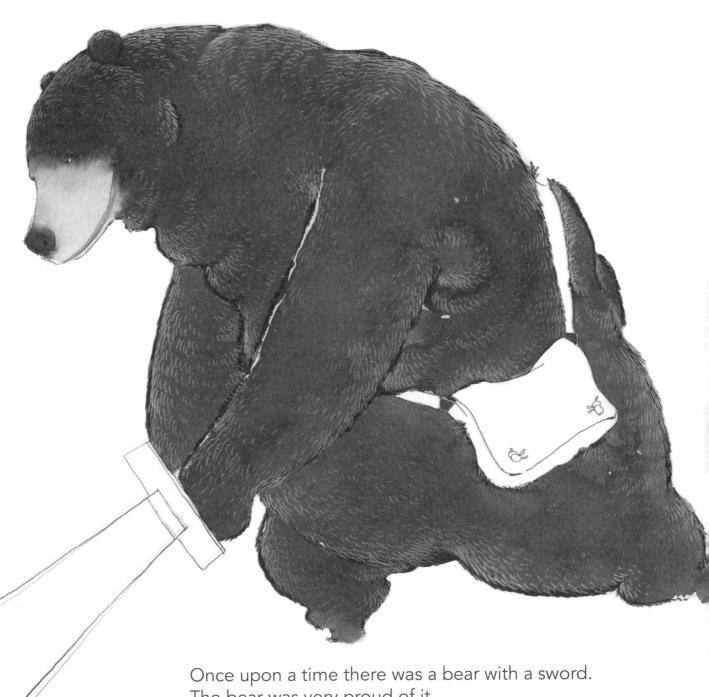

Once upon a time there was a bear with a sword.
The bear was very proud of it.

'My sword can cut through anything,'
he would say.

And to prove it, he just kept on cutting things.

SLASH! SLASH! SLASH!

One day, to prove how powerful his sword was,
he cut down an entire forest,
only stopping when he felt hungry.

Now, the bear lived in a fortress.
He had built it himself to keep out
any enemies who might come along.

The fortress might keep out enemies,
but it couldn't keep out water.

Suddenly, early one morning, water came gushing in.

The bear was furious.

'I'll find out who did this and cut him in two with my sword,' he said.

Then he marched to the dam from where the water was coming.

'There you are!' he shouted to the keepers of the dam. 'You have destroyed my fortress. Now I must cut you in two.'

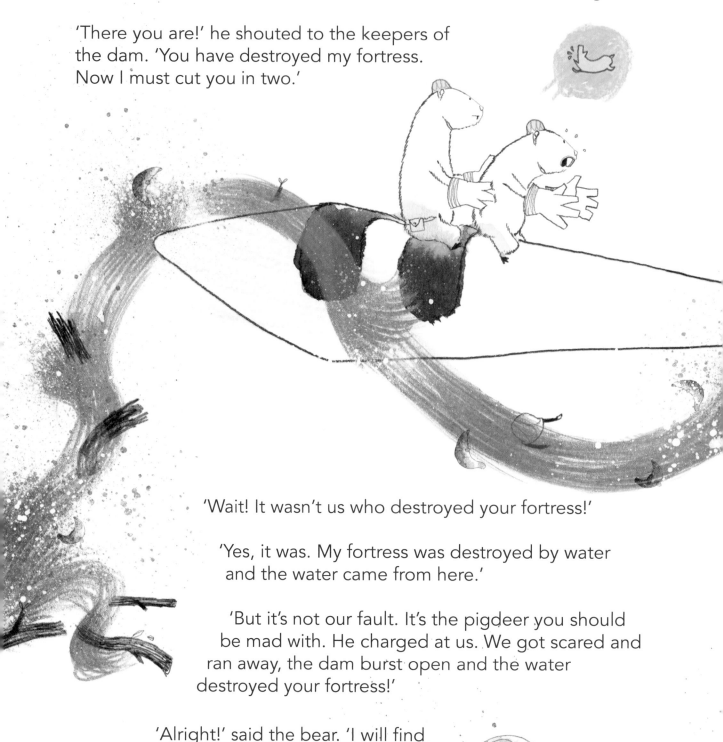

'Wait! It wasn't us who destroyed your fortress!'

'Yes, it was. My fortress was destroyed by water and the water came from here.'

'But it's not our fault. It's the pigdeer you should be mad with. He charged at us. We got scared and ran away, the dam burst open and the water destroyed your fortress!'

'Alright!' said the bear. 'I will find the pigdeer and cut him in two instead.'

'He is easy to recognise: he only has one ear,' said the keepers of the dam.

The pigdeer was lying on the ground, moaning.
It was indeed easy to recognise him because of his missing ear.

'You are the pigdeer who destroyed my fortress,
so I am going to cut you in two.'

'You're wrong. I didn't destroy anything,' said the pigdeer.

'Yes, you did. You scared the keepers of the dam, who ran away
and let the dam burst open, and the water destroyed my fortress!'

'But it's not my fault. It's the fox you should be mad with.
I was sitting quietly when, all of a sudden—ZIP!—
an arrow cut my ear off! Then—ZIP! again—another arrow
stuck in my bottom! I ran to get help but couldn't find any.
That's what really happened!'

'Alright!' said the bear.
'I will find the fox and cut her in two instead.'

'She is easy to recognise: she has one blue eye
and one brown one,' said the pigdeer.

The fox was sitting in front of her house.
The bear drew his sword and said,
'You have destroyed my fortress so now I must cut you in two.'

'You must be confused,' said the lady fox. 'I'm so weak
I couldn't even pull up a bucket of water from the well.
How could I destroy a fortress?'

'And yet you did. You shot arrows at the pigdeer,
who scared the keepers of the dam,
who let the dam burst open, and the water destroyed my fortress!'

'But it's not my fault,' said the fox. 'It was the birds.
They flew in and ate all my fruit! I tried to scare them away
with this old bow and arrows but the arrows shot all over the place.
Then, everything else happened. You should be mad with the
birds: they're the ones who destroyed your fortress.'

'Alright then!' said the bear.
'I'll find them and cut them in two. One by one.'

The bear found the birds.

'You have destroyed my fortress.
Now I must cut every single one of you in two.'

'You're wrong,' said one of them.
'We didn't destroy any fortress.'

'Yes, you did. You ate the fruit that belonged to the fox,
she shot arrows at you which hit the pigdeer,
the pigdeer scared the keepers of the dam,
who let the dam burst open,
and its water destroyed my fortress.'

'But that's not our fault. We were sitting in our trees
when suddenly—WHAM!—they all fell down.
Somebody in the wood cut down all the trees.
You should get mad with them if you don't have a home any more.'

'Alright!' said the bear.
'I'll find him and cut him in two instead.'

The bear looked around and saw all the fallen trees.
Suddenly, he realised it was the forest
he had chopped down earlier with his sword.

The birds, who had followed him there, said
'See? We told you the truth.
Now you have to find the one who did all this
and cut *him* in two with your sword!'

The bear finally understood
that no-one was going to
be cut in two by his sword
unless he cut himself in two.

So he went back to the keepers of the dam.

'Here is my shield,' he said.
'Now you won't be as scared
if you happen to meet another pigdeer!'

Then he went to the pigdeer.

'Be brave. I'm going to
remove the arrow from
your bottom. I'm afraid
it's going to hurt a bit.'

Then the bear bought
some fruit from the market
and took it to the fox.

'You'll have to be patient,'
he said to her.
'Eat this fruit while
you wait for more fruit
to grow on your trees.'

Then the bear planted some new seeds
at the place where the trees
had been cut down.

'You must be patient too,'
he said to the birds.

'These seeds are small now but they will grow.
In the meantime, you can come and live with me.'

And, with that, he took up his sword
and began chopping up the fallen trees
to make a brand new house.

A big house, full of little cubbyholes
for the birds to make their nests in.